PONTYPOOL

Also by Tony Burgess:

The Hellmouths of Bewdley
Pontypool Changes Everything
Caesarea
Fiction for Lovers: A Small Bouquet of Flesh, Fear, Larvae, and Love
Ravenna Gets
People Live Still In Cashtown Corners
Idaho Winter
The n-Body Problem

PONTYPOOL
TONY BURGESS

PLAYWRIGHTS CANADA PRESS
TORONTO

LIBRARY AND ARCHIVES CANADA CATALOGUING IN PUBLICATION
Burgess, Tony, 1959-, author
     Pontypool / Tony Burgess.

Original play of the Pontypool story.
Issued in print and electronic formats.
ISBN 978-1-77091-442-1 (paperback).--ISBN 978-1-77091-443-8 (pdf).
--ISBN 978-1-77091-444-5 (epub).--ISBN 978-1-77091-445-2 (mobi)

     I. Title.

PS8553.U63614P59 2015   C812'.54   C2015-904072-8
                                                  C2015-904073-6

We acknowledge the financial support of the Canada Council for the Arts, the Ontario Arts Council (OAC), the Ontario Media Development Corporation, and the Government of Canada through the Canada Book Fund for our publishing activities. Nous remercions l'appui financier du Conseil des Arts du Canada, le Conseil des arts de l'Ontario (CAO), la Société de développement de l'industrie des médias de l'Ontario, et le Gouvernement du Canada par l'entremise du Fonds du livre du Canada pour nos activités d'édition.

Canada Council   Conseil des arts
for the Arts   du Canada

ONTARIO ARTS COUNCIL
CONSEIL DES ARTS DE L'ONTARIO
an Ontario government agency
un organisme du gouvernement de l'Ontario

Canada

Ontario
Ontario Media Development
Corporation

For Carlyle Edwards and Helen Bonaparte.

Pontypool was directed by Gregory J. Sinclair as a radio drama for CBC Radio in 2009 and starred Stephen McHattie as Grant Mazzy, Lisa Houle as Sydney Briar, Georgina Reilly as Laurel Ann, Rick Roberts as Ken Loney, Hrant Alianak as Dr. Mendez, and Daniel Fathers as Nigel Healing.

The radio drama was adapted for the stage and first produced by Strawdog Theatre Company in Chicago, Illinois, from October 13 to November 4, 2012.

CHARACTERS

Grant Mazzy
Sydney Briar
Laurel Ann Drummond
Ken Loney
Dr. Mendez
Nigel Healing

Black.

We hear a radio tuning in.

GRANT MAZZY: *(on radio)* Welcome back, folks, and good morning from the snow-covered church on the street they call Drum. I've always been a fan of coincidences and when I spot them I make it a hobby of breaking them down, and I'll tell ya, when you look really closely at the fabric of our world, at the details that weave things together, some pretty strange material appears in the most common of events.

The radio signal fuzzes slightly and a few flakes of snow fall in the dark.

Take the bizarre case of Mrs. French's missing cat. You may even have seen the signs she posted all over town. The sad missing posters asking us all if we had seen poor, poor Honey. An all-too-common thing, really, but this case, as it turns out, has a few uncommon twists. Consider the fateful morning Ms. Colette Piscine swerves her car to miss a cat as she goes across a bridge and has to get fished, alive and shivering, out of the drink.

As the radio fuzz continues to come in and out, so the snow appears to fall, seemingly linked. Snow as sound and sight.

This bridge, you may know, is the pride of Caesarea and even has its own fancy name: Pont de Flaque. Now pay attention, folks, 'cause here we go: Colette sounds like *culotte*—panty in French—and *piscine* means pool. Pantypool. *Flaque* also means pool in French. So *Colette Piscine*—in French, Panty Pool—drives over the Pont De Flaque—the *pont de pool*, if you will—to avoid hitting Mrs. French's cat, that has been missing in Pontypool. I mean, it makes my head spin. What does it mean? What does it mean, I hear you ask? Really, it means I have a worn-out French–English dictionary, but it brings an interesting point, and I cite the late great Norman Mailer. God rest the great man. Mailer had an interesting theory he used to explain the strange coincidences in the aftermath of the JFK assassination, which, of course, fuelled conspiracy. In the wake of huge events, after them and before them, physical details spasm for a moment, sort of unlock, and when they come back into focus they suddenly coincide in a weird way. Street names and birthdates and middle names, all kinds of superfluous things appear related to each other.

The radio fuzz grows louder and a heavy blast of snow fills the blackness.

That means something's going to happen. Something big. Something is always about to happen. And that, friends, is another slice of "Isn't It Ironic?"

WOMAN'S VOICE: *(voice-over)* CLSY Beacon Radio! Your Beacon on the Region! You're listening to *Mazzy in the Morning* with your host Grant Mazzy.

GRANT MAZZY is behind a microphone inside a sound booth. On the other side of the booth's glass partition is the control area, where SYDNEY and LAUREL sit.

SYDNEY indicates to GRANT that he's live as the on-air light blinks red. GRANT takes a sip of his coffee, closes his eyes, then leans into the microphone.

GRANT MAZZY: Good morning, Pontypool. You're listening to 660 Radio. The Beacon. Down here in the Dungeon under the street they call Drum. I'm Grant Mazzy and I'll be bangin' the drum all mornin' for ya, and as always taking no prisoners. I got my coffee here and taking a look outside I'd say that's our story for today, folks. I had a strange experience on the drive here and I'm gonna get some advice from you people a little later. When do you call 911? Think about it. I should mention, our producer, the lovely and talented Ms. Sydney Briar is here. And Lucky Laurel Ann Drummond is our technical cowgirl today. And I should also mention—I didn't know this, maybe you did already but this is news to me—Laurel Ann did a tour of duty in Afghanistan not too, too long ago.

LAUREL ANN looks up beaming. SYDNEY rolls her eyes.

SYDNEY BRIAR: *(on air)* You're right, new guy; everybody does know. She was the Grand Master of last year's fall fair. Yesterday's news.

LAUREL ANN: *(on air)* Hey!

SYDNEY BRIAR: *(on air)* Sorry, Laurel Ann. I didn't mean—

LAUREL ANN: *(on air)* I wasn't the Grand Master. I was the Homecoming Hero.

SYDNEY BRIAR: *(on air)* Sorry. Okay. I'm very bad.

GRANT MAZZY: Sydney. Sydney. Sydney. C'mon, girl!

SYDNEY BRIAR: *(on air)* I know; I'm sorry. Sorry.

LAUREL ANN: *(on air)* It's okay. Ms. Briar.

GRANT MAZZY: Call her Sydney. Right, Syd?

> SYDNEY *signals* GRANT *to go to their first story. We hear breaking-news theme music.* GRANT *plays the mechanical drumming monkey.*

In our top story today, a big, cold, dark, white, dull, empty, never-ending, blow-my-brains-out, seasonal-affective disorder, freakin' kill-me-now weather front that'll last all day. The thermometer is headed to minus thirty-two but it's gonna feel like minus forty-two, folks, and that's a dangerous cold. We got an Alberta clipper riding arctic air over the lower lakes so the conditions are good for dark and cold all day. Hopefully when the wind shifts we can get a little greenhouse gas relief from the industrial south. Hail Mary, yea though I walk, we go to Ken Loney in the Sunshine Chopper.

We hear a music cue and the throb of helicopter rotors.

KEN LONEY: *(voice-over)* It's always brighter above the clouds, Grant.

GRANT MAZZY: Hey, Ken, you gonna stay in that bird while the storm rolls in?

KEN LONEY: *(voice-over)* Yessir. Yessiree.

GRANT MAZZY: Is that safe? That can't be safe.

KEN LONEY: *(voice-over)* I'll be up here, Grant, on storm watch, watching all the routes in and around our region.

GRANT MAZZY: Really?

KEN LONEY: Really.

GRANT MAZZY: Okay. If you say so, Ken. I wouldn't wanna be a bird if this storm hits like it's supposed to.

> *KEN continues his traffic report under as the on-air light turns off.*

> *SYDNEY sneezes.*

SYDNEY BRIAR: *(to GRANT)* Leave Ken alone.

LAUREL ANN: I think he's just concerned.

KEN's report comes to an end as SYDNEY smiles then blows her nose. She plays the breaking-news music and cues GRANT as the on-air light blinks on again.

GRANT MAZZY: Thank you, Ken Loney. Breaking news out of Caesarea this morning. OPP are reporting the major bust of a significant grow operation in a quiet cul-de-sac in that town. Constable Howard Ng says it's a sign of things to come.

LAUREL ANN cues the pre-tape of CONSTABLE NG, shooting her finger at GRANT as GRANT shoots back.

LAUREL ANN sneezes.

CONSTABLE NG: *(voie-over)* These operations in suburban small-town neighborhoods are the grow method of choice and supply the drug market with a huge percentage of the supply . . .

CONSTABLE NG's interview continues under as the on-air light turns off.

SYDNEY and LAUREL ANN prepare the next pre-tape as GRANT chats off-air.

GRANT MAZZY: You smoke pot, Syd?

SYDNEY BRIAR: Yes, I do. And stop making jokes about global warming.

GRANT MAZZY: Who made a joke? I quoted the Bible. There are no jokes in the Bible. And speaking of bibles, we're in a church, not a dungeon.

LAUREL ANN holds up her fingers giving an "in five" cue.

The on-air light goes on.

Thanking yew, Constable Howard Ng of the Ontario Provincial Police in Caesarea. Our local pot-growers are engaged in a deadly serious business. Deadly booby traps protecting their operations from prying eyes. Land mines have been found in backyards.

SYDNEY talks to GRANT through his earpiece.

SYDNEY BRIAR: *(in ear)* Cool it, Grant.

GRANT ignores SYDNEY's direction.

GRANT MAZZY: They have vicious attack dogs and there is enough weaponry to arm a small country. These are family neighborhoods. Junior throws a ball through one of these windows and he might just trigger a death squad.

SYDNEY puts a hand to her face.

SYDNEY BRIAR: *(in ear)* What are you doing?

GRANT MAZZY: My producer Sydney is talking in my ear. You can't hear her.

SYDNEY BRIAR: *(in ear)* Nobody cares, Grant, about your gonzo horseshit. You forgot the school closures in the billboard. I'll need you to read the closures.

GRANT MAZZY: Syd says nobody cares. Maybe not. But I think you do, Region. You know what no prisoners means? Full disclosure, whatever the consequences.

SYDNEY BRIAR: *(in ear)* Grant, not full disclosure, school closures. That is what people need.

GRANT MAZZY: Really, Syd. Really. Am I? Am I really?

> *SYDNEY cuts GRANT off and punches up the pre-taped Radio Ray Kowalchuk Sports, which continues under.*

You can't just cut me off like that. Jesus.

> *LAUREL ANN looks uncomfortable. SYDNEY takes a breath.*

SYDNEY BRIAR: Look, Grant. The whole take-no-prisoners shtick works in a bigger context.

GRANT MAZZY: Actually, it's how I got fired.

SYDNEY BRIAR: There's that too, but listen. Small towns already come without prisoners. It's called gossip and its way ahead of you.

GRANT MAZZY: I'm not talking about gossip. I'm talking about building some kind of relationship with listeners. Shaking them up a bit.

SYDNEY BRIAR: We do news, weather, sports, and local spots. That's what we need you to do. What the hell do you think you're going to disclose? What's the big thing you think we need to hear from you?

Pause. GRANT doesn't know how to answer.

GRANT MAZZY: I don't know. Well, no, I do know, Syd. I'm tryin' to piss a few people off, 'cause that's how it's done. Simple as that. A pissed-off listener is a wide-awake listener and he's not gonna change that station; in fact, he's gonna get his pissed-off brother to listen and he's gonna get his pissed-off . . . preacher to listen . . . and . . . that, Lady Briar, is exactly how you build a loyal listening audience.

SYDNEY BRIAR: Well, that sounds perfectly pleasant, I'm sure, and you are first-rate . . . doing a first-rate job, but I'm gonna tell you something. Small towns . . . oh god . . . small towns . . . are not what you think . . . whatever it is you think, but small towns are proud, sometimes fiercely proud places, and so if you come in here, new guy . . . and start lippin' off about taking no prisoners this and pissin' everybody off there, people are gonna think you are just a dick.

GRANT MAZZY: Okay, okay.

SYDNEY BRIAR: You are just going to alienate and embarrass.

GRANT MAZZY: Okay. I said okay.

SYDNEY BRIAR: I'm sorry, it's just the reality. Just go slower. I want Mazziness. I hired Mazziness, but you have to just let the Mazziness slow . . . get to know . . . I don't know what.

GRANT MAZZY: No. I get it. I'm not stupid.

SYDNEY BRIAR: That's not what I meant.

GRANT sits, waiting to return to the air.

LAUREL ANN: I wanted to hear what he was going to say.

SYDNEY BRIAR: He didn't have anything to say. He was just going to talk about himself.

SYDNEY cues GRANT as the on-air light comes on.

GRANT MAZZY: Pontypool, my Pontypool. We interrupt our call-in segment to bring you breaking news out of our area this morning. Out on Sandy Hook and Wilmont, we have a hostage situation. Two men are holding a van load of people at gunpoint. The van is apparently towing a fishing hut.

GRANT smirks. SYDNEY motions for GRANT to put in his earpiece.

(fitting in his earpiece) Sporadic gunfire has been reported. OPP constables Bob Roseland and Derek McCormack are on the scene.

SYDNEY speaks to GRANT through an earpiece.

SYDNEY BRIAR: *(in ear)* Lose the story, Grant. I'll get Ken. We're going to the Sunshine Chopper.

GRANT MAZZY: *(reading the wire)* No one knows as yet what these hostage-takers want or whether or not they know the people in the van . . .

SYDNEY BRIAR: *(in ear)* They're all drunk, Grant. It's the end of the ice-fishing season.

GRANT MAZZY: . . . but being the end of the ice-fishing season— ice hut removal time—the chances that everyone on the ice this morning is drunk—is a very distinct reality. Drunk ice fishermen and, dare I say, drunk policemen. Drunk officers of the law. Drunk Ontario Provincial Police. This is not yet confirmed by our sources, but . . .

(reading the wire) . . . police . . . possibly drunk . . . are reporting that the hostage situation has resolved itself. They have two suspects in custody, both UNARMED as it turns out, and the three people they were holding have in fact fled the scene. One can only hope that breaking news theme music will accompany this story at some point.

SYDNEY BRIAR: *(in ear)* Wrap it up, Grant.

GRANT MAZZY: The state of drunkenness has levelled off to acceptable levels this morning as Buddy Bob Roseland and Deadeye Derek McCormack, OPP Pontypool division, have contained the "hostage" situation. We'll be back with updates as the situation hiccups. We now go to Ken Loney in the Sunshine Chopper to lend a little perspective to your morning drive. And that's my day, your mornin' man. Grant Mazzy, freakin' at the beacon. Have a good one and keep an eye out for crazy ladies in the snow. Drive safe.

LAUREL ANN flips the switches to get KEN LONEY *on the air.* KEN *continues under through the following scene.*

SYDNEY looks at GRANT, *frustrated.*

I'm sorry. I thought it was funny.

SYDNEY's shoulders fall.

I'm sorry. Look, you people gotta learn to laugh at yourselves every once in a while.

SYDNEY BRIAR: The story is not funny. Derek McCormack is an alcoholic. Bob Roseland is an alcoholic. They are trying to keep their jobs. Derek is my brother-in-law. Ex-brother-in-law.

SYDNEY takes a breath.

GRANT MAZZY: Oh. Ouch. How was I supposed to know?

SYDNEY BRIAR: Ken Loney is not in a chopper.

GRANT MAZZY: What?

SYDNEY BRIAR: The Sunshine Chopper is Ken's Dodge Dart. He plays sound effects.

GRANT MAZZY: Wow.

SYDNEY BRIAR: Okay?

GRANT MAZZY: Okay.

SYDNEY BRIAR: Ken sits up on a hill for his aerial view. In his car all day. For us. Okay?

GRANT MAZZY: Aerial view?

SYDNEY BRIAR: Aerial view, Grant. And people who listen to him are happy to have him up there flying around in the Sunshine Chopper even though.

GRANT MAZZY: Okay.

SYDNEY BRIAR: Okay.

GRANT MAZZY: Uh, Syd . . .

SYDNEY BRIAR: Yeah?

GRANT MAZZY: I hate winter.

SYDNEY BRIAR: Everybody does.

GRANT MAZZY: Not like me. These late winters, I feel like I live in the basement of the world. So cold. Dark . . .

SYDNEY BRIAR: Yup.

GRANT MAZZY: Yessir.

SYDNEY BRIAR: You'll be okay.

GRANT MAZZY: Yeah. Anyway. That's me done for today. Where's Roger Moore?

SYDNEY BRIAR: Uh. I need to ask you something. A favour. Roger Moore didn't show up. I can't reach him. Could you fill in for him?

GRANT MAZZY: Me be Roger Moore?

SYDNEY BRIAR: I know. I know. Not exactly your kettle, but I'm in a jam, honey.

GRANT MAZZY: You owe me.

SYDNEY BRIAR: Tell you what. When this fish hut story gets corroborated we'll get to you right away. Right away. It's yours and if it turns out to not be real then you can take no prisoners with it, whatever you want.

> *The breaking-news theme music plays as the on-air light switches on.* GRANT *smiles. He comes to life as he reads from* SYDNEY's *notes.*

GRANT MAZZY: We have breaking news in the region this morning. It seems that a large group of people have gathered outside the office of Dr. John Mendez. It appears to be a protest of some kind and officials are describing the crowd as unruly. Dr. Mendez, you may recall, was under investigation last year for writing unnecessary prescriptions. We have an exclusive live report from Ken Loney in the . . . Sunshine Chopper. Ken, what can you see?

GRANT *looks up at* SYDNEY. *She glares back, mouthing, "Don't you dare."*

KEN LONEY: *(voice-over)* Grant. I am watching hundreds, literally hundreds of people packed in and around this building. It looks pretty odd from up here. They seem to be trying to cram themselves inside. Oh! Oh!

GRANT MAZZY: What's happening, Ken?

KEN LONEY: *(voice-over)* Oh! The side of the office . . . this building has just burst outward, spilling people. It just kind of exploded. Oh! Jesus! It looks like an explosion . . . of people. Oh god! People are getting trampled. What are they doing? People are getting killed down there. Oh!

GRANT MAZZY: Ken, do you see any police? Is anybody trying to restore order . . . "down there"?

KEN LONEY: *(voice-over)* No. No. I don't see . . . wait. There's a line . . . like a convoy of trucks . . . military vehicles. Where did they come from? What the hell? Helicopters. There's a helicopter at my two o'clock and one . . . I gotta back up outta here. Holy shit, the road is blocked.

GRANT *looks back at* SYDNEY. SYDNEY *shakes her head.*

GRANT MAZZY: Get safe, Ken. Get out of there.

KEN LONEY: *(voice-over)* There's definitely fatalities here. Down there. People have just died, Grant. I don't know what the hell just happened.

GRANT MAZZY: Well. We're . . . we're gonna have to see if we can . . . Ken!? Ken, are you there!?!

SYDNEY and LAUREL ANN frantically check their equipment, trying to get KEN back on air. They check the news wire for more information.

SYDNEY BRIAR: *(in ear)* I have nothing on the wire, Grant.

LAUREL ANN picks up the phone to call the police.

GRANT MAZZY: . . . get some information on what is clearly happening . . .

SYDNEY BRIAR: *(in ear)* Christ, this is happening five miles from here.

GRANT MAZZY: . . . Not more than three miles from this station itself. This is what we have. We have . . .

SYDNEY BRIAR: *(in ear)* Don't say a lot, Grant. We need to get this confirmed somehow.

GRANT MAZZY: . . . Something has happened at a doctor's office here in Pontypool involving a possible riot . . .

The on-air light blinks out as SYDNEY cuts to a pre-taped segment.

SYDNEY BRIAR: I'm sorry, Grant. I know you wanted to stay with the story, but we just had to buy some time and I appreciate it. I really do. And we have something and I'm throwin' it all back to you. Now.

GRANT MAZZY: Oh. Okay. Really? Okay. What do we got?

SYDNEY BRIAR: Well, Laurel Ann says there's still nothing anywhere on any wire, but we've got ten confirmations from various eyewitnesses in town. We're going on with Steve VanDenzen. He's an eyewitness. He's good.

GRANT MAZZY: That's great. Fuck the wire if we got eyes.

SYDNEY BRIAR: Keep it hot, Grant.

GRANT MAZZY: You know it, girl. Hit me.

GRANT ducks behind his microphone and reads what SYDNEY has sent to his monitor.

SYDNEY BRIAR: *(to LAUREL ANN)* Any word from Ken?

LAUREL ANN: Nothing.

The breaking-news theme music plays as the on-air light comes back on.

GRANT MAZZY: Welcome back to our developing story where it appears that hundreds of people have been involved in a riot in and around the office of Dr. John Mendez. You heard our own Ken Loney describe the violent scene only minutes ago. We take you now live to eyewitness Steve VanDenzen. Steve?

We hear a background of chaos, moans, and screams.

STEVE VANDENZEN: *(voice-over)* Prah.

GRANT MAZZY: Steve? Steve VanDenzen!?

STEVE VANDENZEN: *(voice-over)* Prah. Prah.

GRANT looks bewildered. He looks at SYDNEY, who cuts the live feed.

SYDNEY BRIAR: *(in ear)* Grant! Grant! Frankie from Cyril's has confirmed that . . .

GRANT MAZZY: We have just had a report from a Pontypool resident that confirms . . .

SYDNEY BRIAR: *(in ear)* . . . a crowd of people had gathered near Cyril's hardware store . . . and made their way to the office of Dr. Mendez . . .

GRANT MAZZY: . . . Indeed a mob was spotted moving through town toward the doctor's office. We are still waiting to learn what exactly motivated this crowd, this mob . . .

SYDNEY BRIAR: *(in ear)* Um . . . The resident says that . . . shit . . . don't say this, Grant . . .

GRANT MAZZY: . . . To organize in a seemingly spontaneous fashion, gathering in numbers as it went . . .

SYDNEY BRIAR: *(in ear)* Somebody's messing with us, Grant.

GRANT MAZZY: It is hard to get a fix on what has happened, but, clearly, you heard our reporter Ken Loney earlier . . .

SYDNEY BRIAR: *(in ear)* . . . I know, Grant. I don't know. We can't reach Ken. This is really fucked. I don't know what's going on . . .

GRANT MAZZY: . . . And we're trying to reach him.

SYDNEY BRIAR: *(in ear)* Wrap it, Grant.

GRANT MAZZY: Please stay tuned to our developing story as the crisis at the offices of Dr. Mendez unfolds.

> *GRANT looks up to see the on-air light is still on. He looks to* SYDNEY *and* LAUREL ANN *in the control booth; they are both busy on separate phones.* SYDNEY *eventually notices the dead air and waves at* GRANT *and then points to the on-air light.* GRANT, *irritated, shrugs and leans into the microphone.* SYDNEY *punches in the breaking-news theme song.*

Good afternoon. This is CLSY 660. Beacon Radio. I'm Grant Mazzy coming to you live from the church on Drum. A drum we are banging with great alarm here this afternoon. It has been some time since today's bizarre mob assault on the offices of Dr. Mendez. We still do not have an official version of these events, but it has been reported that up to seventy-five people are dead and at least twice that number are injured.

SYDNEY BRIAR: *(in ear)* That's good. That sounds honest. That is honest. I have CBC and CFRB wanting to talk to you on-air.

GRANT looks very pleased with this news.

GRANT MAZZY: Police are not commenting on the condition of the victims but say that the brutality has been "alarming and unacceptable."

SYDNEY BRIAR: *(in ear)* That's a stupid thing to say. Sorry. You didn't say it. The police did. Sorry.

GRANT MAZZY: An eyewitness account has described this morning's events as the "biblically aberrant behaviour of the citizenry of Pontypool." We now have Constable Bob Roseland of the Pontypool unit of the OPP on the line live. Constable Roseland, what's happening out there?

BOB ROSELAND: *(voice-over)* At seven o'clock this morning our officers answered a 911 call to the Golden Dawn facility to discover a large number of people occupying the building. They seemed to be trying to get to an elderly woman's room. This woman has since died from incidental injuries as a result of people piling into her room.

SYDNEY BRIAR: *(in ear)* They were all chanting the same thing, Grant. They were chanting something. This is so fucking creepy. Ask Roseland about . . .

GRANT MAZZY: What were they saying?

BOB ROSELAND: *(voice-over)* They were repeating things this woman was saying. And she's all senile so she's babbling about Hitler and some hurricane that killed her father and . . .

SYDNEY BRIAR: *(in ear)* That's crazy talk, Grant. Get out.

> *SYDNEY cuts off ROSELAND's feed and points to GRANT's monitor. GRANT leans back into his microphone.*

GRANT MAZZY: Thank you, Constable Roseland.

We are also hearing about a herd—that's how it's being described—a herd of people at the edge of the forest off Highway 26 near Edenvale. That's northwest of us, and between here and there in Phelpston a man and his two children are trapped in their car, which is under a pile, a mountain of people. Police say they haven't actually been able to see the car for over an hour. Bugs. They sound like bugs.

> *LAUREL ANN answers a call. She lights up, trying to get SYDNEY's attention.*

SYDNEY BRIAR: *(in ear)* These people were listening to windshield wipers. We can't report this stuff. I don't know. I've got a Rachel Jones telling me that these people were talking to the windshield wipers. Imitating the noise they were making. She's acting very weird. She isn't making any sense.

GRANT MAZZY: There are a growing number of eyewitness accounts but still we have had nothing like a press conference or official statement . . .

LAUREL ANN: Sydney. *BBC World News* is on the line.

SYDNEY BRIAR: BBC?

LAUREL ANN nods seriously.

(in ear) Grant. I've got Nigel Healing for you.

GRANT MAZZY: What?

SYDNEY BRIAR: *(in ear)* Don't talk to me! Nigel Healing. *BBC World News*, Grant. He wants to interview you on air. Their air and our air.

GRANT MAZZY: Let's just do it!

LAUREL ANN streams the audio from BBC World News *on her computer and we hear* NIGEL HEALING, *a distinguished British radio voice.*

NIGEL HEALING: We are talking to Grant Mazzy, the news radio anchor from Pontypool, Ontario, in Canada, who broke this story. Mr. Mazzy, are you there?

GRANT MAZZY: Yes, Nigel. Hi. Nigel.

NIGEL HEALING: Mr. Mazzy. Is it true that French-Canadian soldiers have set up roadblocks preventing people from leaving and entering your area? And if so, does this have anything to do with your country's history of separatist terror groups?

> *SYDNEY and LAUREL ANN look baffled. As NIGEL HEALING continues, SYDNEY speaks into GRANT's ear.*

SYDNEY BRIAR: *(in ear)* No. I haven't heard any of this, Grant. I don't think he knows what he's talking about.

GRANT MAZZY: Nigel, none of that is true. The military is rumoured to be involved, and the local police are responding as we speak . . . There is nothing in these events that suggest that there is anything political or even organized, certainly not terrorist or separatist.

NIGEL HEALING: But, Mr. Mazzy, this certainly looks like an insurgency of some kind. Large groups of people are involved. If it's not organized and it's not political then can you help our viewers at home understand what it is exactly that we have been reporting on?

SYDNEY BRIAR: *(in ear)* He's good.

GRANT MAZZY: Nigel, the honest truth is that no one has officially come out ahead of this. We do not know.

NIGEL HEALING: There you have it. A series of strange riots and violent mob scenes in rural Canada that no one, I repeat, no one, can explain. Meanwhile reports persist that French-Canadian riot police have been called in to crush this insurgency.

NIGEL continues under as LAUREL ANN picks up the phone and starts pointing excitedly toward GRANT.

SYDNEY BRIAR: *(in ear)* Fuck you, Nigel Healing. He knows nothing.

LAUREL ANN: I got Ken!

SYDNEY quickly cuts off NIGEL's audio feed and cues the breaking-news theme music.

GRANT MAZZY: That was Nigel Healing from our affiliate station, BBC. We now go to Ken Loney, our reporter in the field here in Pontypool. Ken? Are you there, Ken?

KEN LONEY: *(voice-over)* Yes. Yes. I'm here. Send someone. I'm not safe here.

GRANT MAZZY: Not safe where, Ken?

SYDNEY BRIAR: *(in ear)* Don't say where he is. If anything happens to him—

KEN LONEY: *(voice-over)* I'm inside the grain silo near the train tracks. The big silo, not one of the little ones. I ran here from the entranceway of Nimigon National Park. They came after us. You got to send police.

SYDNEY BRIAR: *(in ear)* No police can be reached, Grant. There is no contacting the police.

GRANT MAZZY: Can you describe the scene there?

KEN LONEY: *(voice-over)* Describe . . . it's pitch black. I'm lying in something in the dark.

GRANT MAZZY: Can you tell us what happened? What's happening out there.

KEN LONEY: *(voice-over)* I'll tell you this . . . I just saw . . . I've seen things today that are gonna ruin the rest of my natural life, Grant. I . . . I'm scared . . .

> *GRANT is completely engaged.* KEN *is choked with fear and emotion, unable to speak.*

GRANT MAZZY: Ken? Ken, listen to me. It sounds like you're okay where you are. Don't move, just stay there, and we'll see if we can't send—

KEN LONEY: *(voice-over)* They look like animals. Some were naked. Like dogs. And their eyes. That look. Just a . . . startled and wild . . .

SYDNEY BRIAR: *(in ear)* Oh god, Grant.

GRANT MAZZY: Okay. Ken. Listen, we'll—

KEN LONEY: *(voice-over)* No. You don't understand. I'm looking through a little door. There's a little door at the base of the door, some kinda cat door or something, and I can see . . . let me just move so I can see. Oh! Look out! Oh god! They're pulling two people out of a van and just . . .

GRANT MAZZY: Who are they? Who's "they," Ken?

KEN LONEY: *(voice-over)* There's a bunch of 'em. They're people but they're crazy. They're pulling these two out of the van! Oh my god! They're biting them. They're actually carrying them to the ground in their mouths. This is awful. This is terrible. I can't see . . . they're biting . . . just biting. They look like a school of fish. Like a frenzy, piranha. Almost as if . . . it's as if . . . it's just how it looks I guess but it looks like these people are trying to climb or eat their way inside . . . so desperate, like they have to be inside . . . one has his entire leg and another his arm, right inside . . .

SYDNEY BRIAR: *(in ear)* Stop him, Grant. Stop him!

KEN LONEY: *(voice-over)* They're pulling themselves apart. AHHHH! One just pulled his head off and threw it!

SYDNEY BRIAR: *(in ear)* Now! Grant! Stop this now!

> *We hear the sounds of movement, shuffling, frantic, from* KEN's *audio feed.*

KEN LONEY: *(voice-over)* Shit. He heard that. One of them looked over. He heard me. He's coming. Holy shit. I gotta hide. He's running.

SYDNEY BRIAR: Get out of there, Ken!

> *Bang! Bang! Crash! The sound of splintering wood then a terrible moan.*

> *Silence.*

> *GRANT sounds as if he's coming out of a trance. He is, in fact, in shock.*

GRANT MAZZY: Ken? Ken. It's Grant. Are you injured? Have you been injured?

KEN LONEY: *(voice-over)* No. No. I'm just lying here in the dark. It crashed through the wall. It was Mary Gault's boy. Her big teenager. Jesse or Jake or something. It was him. He had no hands. Kid had no hands.

SYDNEY BRIAR: *(in ear)* Stop him, Grant. Stop him.

GRANT MAZZY: What's he doing now?

KEN LONEY: *(voice-over)* I can see him. He's looking at me. I think he can't move. He must have broken some bones. I can see his eyes. He can't move. I think he's . . . hang on.

GRANT MAZZY: Ken? Ken? I wouldn't go near him, Ken.

SYDNEY BRIAR: *(in ear)* Not on the air, Grant. I'm not going to listen to somebody get killed on the air.

KEN LONEY: *(voice-over)* He's whispering something. He's saying something. I'm going to get closer and see if I can hear what he's saying.

GRANT MAZZY: I don't know about that, Ken.

> *A tense pause.* GRANT *and* SYDNEY *stare at each other.*
>
> *Crack! Buzz! Snap! A loud voice breaks in.*
>
> GRANT *clutches the microphone.*

Ken? Ken?

LOUD FRENCH VOICE: *(voice-over) Pour votre sécurité, merci d'éviter les contacts avec votre proche famille et éviter ce qui suit: Limiter les charmes, comme mon chou ou un amoureux. Parler bébé avec des enfants en bas âge. Discours rhétorique.*

Merci de ne pas traduire cette annonce.

> *A pause.*

SYDNEY BRIAR: What was that? That cut into our signal.

GRANT MAZZY: Ken? Do we still have Ken?

SYDNEY BRIAR: *(in ear)* No. We lost Ken.

GRANT MAZZY: Folks, we've lost Ken.

SYDNEY BRIAR: Laurel Ann, did you get any of it? Can you translate it?

LAUREL ANN: Workin' on it . . .

GRANT MAZZY: We are working on a translation of the message we just received live on the air.

LAUREL ANN: Something about avoid family members and talk only . . . only talk to babies. Crazy shit.

GRANT MAZZY: The message, an incoherent rambling in French, is likely to be a hoax of some kind. We are, however, working on a translation.

SYDNEY BRIAR: *(in ear)* Recap while we figure it out.

LAUREL ANN: Got it!

SYDNEY BRIAR: *(in ear)* Okay. It's on your screen.

GRANT MAZZY: We have the translation. I'm going to read this, reminding our listeners that the source has not been identified and early analysis describes this as a hoax . . .

SYDNEY BRIAR: *(in ear)* Let me look it over first. Recap, Grant, recap.

GRANT MAZZY: For those of you who have just joined us we have breaking news, to say the least, here in Pontypool and possibly, probably affecting a wider area than we know at this point. Our own Ken Loney is on the ground in a silo near the tracks by Nimigon Park and is under a siege of some kind. We have this story and others as related to us by local police of gangs or groups of people committing awful and perverse, I would say, perverse acts of violence. As a general warning, though we haven't officially heard one yet, we at the station are advising our listeners to stick close to the radio, stay indoors. We have also learned that some of the perpetrators are speaking in bizarre ways, as to whether this is deliberate, a way of terrorizing people, we just don't know. We have something coming in just now, folks, listen up.

This is what that voice, that alarming voice we heard earlier said. And I remind you that the source was not us and, indeed, we do not know the source.

GRANT leans into his microphone as he reads the translation.

For your safety, please avoid contact with close family members and restrain from the following: All terms of endearment such as "honey" or "sweetheart," baby talk with young children, and rhetorical discourse. For greater safety, please avoid the English language. Thank you for not translating this warning.

Pause. KEN's voice chimes back in. They all become alert.

KEN LONEY: *(voice-over)* Did you get that?

GRANT MAZZY: Hello? Is someone there? Hello?

LAUREL ANN: It's Ken!

GRANT MAZZY: Ken! Ken! Thank god!

SYDNEY BRIAR: *(in ear)* Ken! Ken!

KEN LONEY: *(voice-over)* Did you get that?

GRANT MAZZY: I don't know, Ken. I can't say I actually GET anything right this second.

KEN LONEY: *(voice-over)* Okay. Let's try that again. Listen. Keep in mind—picture this. This, what you're about to hear, is coming from Mary Gault's boy. Lying here in the dark with his body broken to pieces and his wrists, I can see them, stumps. Gnawed stumps pointing up at his sides.

SYDNEY BRIAR: *(in ear)* No, no, Grant. What are we doing now?

KEN LONEY: *(voice-over)* Listen. Shhh.

A rustling sound. Then a raspy voice. Then inside that raspy voice, the clear sound of a baby screaming.

BABY'S RASPY VOICE: *(voice-over)* Mommy! Help me! Mommy!

KEN LONEY: *(voice-over)* Did you hear that? I don't even know how he's doing that. It sounds like there's a child screaming inside his breath.

Silence.

Are you guys still there? Hello?

GRANT MAZZY: Is this actually happening?

SYDNEY BRIAR: *(in ear)* Easy, Grant. Easy. We have to . . . shit. Shit.

GRANT MAZZY: That was . . . that was Ken Loney interviewing a . . . screaming baby trapped in Mary Gault's oldest boy's last dying gasps . . .

> *GRANT leans over. He appears dizzy, blinking, not speaking into the microphone.*

That is what . . . how a little baby can be . . . a baby's voice . . .

> *He is swooning.*

SYDNEY BRIAR: *(in ear)* Nigel Healing is talking about the cat, Grant. He just said "Honey." He's talking about people carrying that cat poster.

GRANT MAZZY: He what?

SYDNEY BRIAR: *(in ear)* The Honey the cat poster. Honey the missing cat! Grant? Let's get out. School closures in five . . . four . . .

> *The on-air light goes off and the automatic report starts playing. GRANT looks shell-shocked in his booth.*

> *In the control room LAUREL ANN is muttering to herself. She suddenly snaps upright and then stands perfectly still. SYDNEY*

tries to get LAUREL ANN's attention but nothing breaks her focus. Nervously, SYDNEY makes her way into the sound booth. GRANT is sitting, drinking directly from a flask, unaware of LAUREL ANN's bizarre behaviour.

LAUREL ANN stares through the glass, fixated, at GRANT and SYDNEY.

Black.

The lights come back up on GRANT, SYDNEY, and DR. JOHN MENDEZ in the sound booth. The control room appears empty. MENDEZ is dishevelled—his clothes dirtied and torn, as though he barely survived a fight. SYDNEY is applying a bandage to MENDEZ's hand and forearm.

GRANT is at the microphone, already speaking as the lights come up. He is reading the obituaries, extemporizing to heighten the absurd drama of local deaths.

GRANT MAZZY: Gwendoline Parker was taken from this life in her forty-fifth year by her beloved husband Stanley, who left this world suddenly at the hand of family members, Fiona and Michael, who then died at each other's hands in their twelfth and seventeenth years, respectively.

Janice Gwynne has departed from her abiding husband by his own hand in the thirty-fourth year of her life. Jack Gwynne survived long enough to add four names—Paul Hieghton, forty-two; Alice Hieghton, forty-three; Brenda Hieghton, twelve; and young Jesse

Hieghton, ten—to the list of passages before himself losing his life as a result of an accident.

Greg Olan, fifty-six, has been killed by Yolanda Olan, sixty-one, who also removed Freida Olan, eighty-one; Patsy Olan, twelve; John Freethy, thirty-three; Peter Stamp, thirty-eight; and Leslie Reid, forty-two; who had between them caused the untimely passings of Joel Froth, sixty-seven; Sandra Weydon, twenty-three; Tim Drummond, seventeen; Cynthia Drummond, forty-six; Darren Drummond, fifty-one; and Alicia Drummond, ninety-one.

The Drummonds were survived on Cynthia's side by the Hindman family until shortly before noon yesterday when they were sadly removed from this world by a bus driven by the recently departed Brenda Lockland, forty-three, who was missed briefly by her husband, Gary, thirty-seven, now deceased.

> *SYDNEY stands and moves to the glass separating the control room from the sound booth, watching for LAUREL ANN.*

Welcome, folks, you're listening to the Beacon. We are holding our own. No prisoners, friends. Well, today, we ARE those prisoners. WE are tired. We are scared. But we have a special guest. Dr. John Mendez is with us today. You may know him or recall Ken Loney's story earlier as he reported live as a violent mob destroyed his practice. Dr. Mendez has had some special experience with these events and hopefully can give us some insight . . . uh . . .

> *MENDEZ pulls a pill bottle out and takes a pill. SYDNEY stiffens and steps back from the sound booth window. GRANT stops*

*talking but does not move, taking a drink from his flask.
LAUREL ANN appears in the control room. She is notably the
worse for wear—her clothes are dishevelled and torn and she
is showing signs of bodily injury.*

SYDNEY BRIAR: She's . . . Laurel Ann! Laurel Ann! Stop!

DR. MENDEZ: She's routing for voices. This will grow vicious.

Slam! LAUREL ANN slams into the glass and falls.

GRANT is ignoring this and trying to remain steady on the air.

GRANT MAZZY: I should mention that, sadly . . . uh . . . very
sadly . . . Homecoming Hero Laurel Ann Drummond is currently
undergoing some kind of dangerous—I'll call them seizures . . .
uh . . . can she hear us out there? Are the monitors on?

SYDNEY BRIAR: No. They're off. I just saw her. She went on all
fours back behind those bins.

The lights start to flicker on and off.

DR. MENDEZ: She would probably just root around the speakers
anyway. If the sound was on.

GRANT MAZZY: So, is this consistent with what you have observed,
Dr. Mendez? Whoops. I should let you know, folks, Laurel Ann
has been randomly flicking our lights on and off, and though you
can't see this, it's pretty unnerving, and if you hear a gasp or I

seem distracted it's because I keep going from bright bright lights to pitch black. At the whim of a madwoman.

SYDNEY BRIAR: *(whispering)* Don't say that, Grant.

GRANT MAZZY: Go ahead, Dr. Mendez . . .

The lights come on. The three gasp.

And the Good Lord said let there be—

*LAUREL ANN is close to the glass staring. SYDNEY screams.
LAUREL ANN's face is mutilated and imbedded with electronic
bric-a-brac.*

Laurel Ann! Jesus. Oh. Shit. Oh. She doesn't look so good. Folks, uh. Laurel Ann has made an appearance. She's standing at the glass right here. Inches away from us, and she doesn't look good. She looks like she tried maybe to eat something, a . . .

DR. MENDEZ: That might be a radio.

GRANT MAZZY: Okay. But she's got . . .

SYDNEY sobs.

Is that a battery under her teeth there?

SYDNEY BRIAR: Stop, Grant.

LAUREL ANN steps backward and away, leaving the control room.

GRANT MAZZY: There she goes.

SYDNEY BRIAR: There she goes.

GRANT MAZZY: Back to the light. And boom. Dark.

SYDNEY BRIAR: I can't take this.

GRANT MAZZY: Laurel Ann. I love Laurel Ann.

SYDNEY BRIAR: I love Laurel Ann, too.

GRANT MAZZY: Full disclosure, folks. No prisoners. I don't like sitting in dark places.

DR. MENDEZ: Are we doing the radio show?

GRANT MAZZY: Yeah. We are.

DR. MENDEZ: When?

GRANT MAZZY: This is it.

DR. MENDEZ: Of course. They can't see in the dark.

Slam! LAUREL ANN hits the glass walls of the sound booth with ferocity.

All three scream.

Slam! Harder again, this time leaving a slash of blood across the glass.

Scream!

SYDNEY BRIAR: I can't see anything! Where is she? Where is she?

GRANT MAZZY: Okay. Okay. Let's just take a breath. She can't get in. Let's get Dr. Mendez to chime in here. You have some familiarity with this . . . what is it? . . . this . . .

DR. MENDEZ: Oh. Nightmare. This is a nightmare and we are all awake for it. I have seen this, what your friend is experiencing. It starts, well, subtle at first. I'm sorry you are horrified. You should be. It's horrible. The first thing you notice is that they will say something . . . something odd . . . something that suggests they aren't apprehending things exactly as you are and then, sometimes quickly sometimes it takes a while, their speech starts to disorganize or, in some cases, hyper organize. Echolalia, aphasia, astonishing mimicry and arguments. The arguing that consists of non sequiturs, this is a deterioration and this is where they become dangerous. They seek organized speech. They start to hunt for us. They want to repeat what we say and worse.

The lights come on, revealing streaks of gore on the glass. Everyone screams. Then they cough and gag in revulsion.

GRANT MAZZY: Sorry. Folks. The lights just came on again. And we can't see Laurel Ann anywhere but there is a lot of blood and . . . that she's left on the glass and it's just hard not to . . .

SYDNEY BRIAR: There she is! She's over by the door.

GRANT MAZZY: Okay. Sorry, folks. Dr. Mendez . . .

DR. MENDEZ: Yes. Uh. The final stage—the stage I have seen— they will hunt for a healthy person—and this sounds very very strange but it is as I say it is—they try to enter speech through the mouth, biting and ripping though the victim's mouth and then diving down, climbing down. I don't know how to describe it, like a frog climbing into a snake's mouth, and they die inside the body of the person they have entered. Over time they will all die from wounds they receive inadvertently from their obsessive actions.

GRANT MAZZY: Unbelievable.

Slam! The blur of LAUREL ANN bangs into the glass booth.

No one screams. Pause.

DR. MENDEZ: Okay? Can I . . . ? Okay. I saw much of this, elements of this in the last week in my practice. I realized in time that if I said nothing I was sort of invisible and that's how I escaped the mob of them. I shut up and I walked away.

Slam! LAUREL ANN hits the glass again and GRANT jumps.

She doesn't have a victim so I'm not sure how this will end. The victim suicides but the victim needs a victim to suicide into.

SYDNEY gives MENDEZ an incredulous look as if he's insane. Her phone rings. MENDEZ sneezes.

SYDNEY BRIAR: I got Ken. Let's go to Ken.

SYDNEY hurriedly sets up her telephone, on speaker, to one of the microphones, then settles back into her chair, pensive.

GRANT MAZZY: Thank you, Dr. Mendez. We now have our field reporter, Ken Loney, on the line from the grain silo in Pontypool. We have our reporter on the line now. Ken? Are you there?

KEN LONEY: *(voice-over)* I'm here, Grant. Ken Loney reporting from inside a grain silo.

GRANT MAZZY: We've been very worried about you, Ken.

KEN LONEY: *(voice-over)* I think I'm okay, but the person who was in here with me has died.

GRANT MAZZY: Have you been there all this time?

KEN LONEY: *(voice-over)* Haven't moved. I can hear crowds from time to time, shuffling past out there.

DR. MENDEZ: Can you hear what they are saying? Are they saying anything?

KEN LONEY: *(voice-over)* I have. You can hear them. A group went by about an hour ago and they were all talking about U-boats. Well, they weren't talking, really, sort of chanting. Something about "Look out for U-boats."

DR. MENDEZ: What the hell is that? The sheer bizarreness of that makes me shiver.

GRANT MAZZY: Were they all saying this, Ken?

KEN LONEY: *(voice-over)* Yeah. All of 'em. It's a simple of the disorder.

DR. MENDEZ: A symbol of the disorder? You mean a symptom?

KEN LONEY: *(voice-over)* It's a simple . . . ummm.

DR. MENDEZ: You know, we've heard about this connection to old people and young people. War vets are old people. Maybe . . . I'm not sure.

KEN LONEY: *(voice-over)* I have a problem.

GRANT MAZZY: What's happening there? Do you have to get somewhere safer?

KEN LONEY: *(voice-over)* No. That's not it.

DR. MENDEZ: People are repeating. Yes. The people in my office this morning. "Honey." It's a kind of comfort. Repetition. It's something the mind seeks as it—

SYDNEY BRIAR: *(whispering)* Is Ken okay?

GRANT MAZZY: You okay, Ken?

KEN LONEY: *(voice-over)* I don't know. I don't think so.

GRANT MAZZY: What's going on?

KEN LONEY: *(voice-over)* This is gonna sound weird. I can't stop thinking . . . "Do you have a sample?"

GRANT MAZZY: I'm sorry? A sample? A sample of what?

KEN LONEY: *(voice-over)* Um . . . just a sample. I think a simple kind of sample. This is what I was saying. I need to . . . Grant?

GRANT MAZZY: I'm here, Ken. What kind of sample are you talking about?

KEN LONEY: *(voice-over)* That's right, that's right. I'll tell you quickly, Grant. Sample right now is where I should go. It doesn't feel safe. I need to mention the sample a lot but I'm still trying to talk. I need to say, "Is the sample ready?" "Sample seems good, there's a lot there." That's, anyway, where I'm at. Very, very far back from saying what you think is easy right now. Can't stop some sample of what I'm trying to say.

GRANT MAZZY: Try to stay calm, Ken.

SYDNEY BRIAR: Oh my god.

DR. MENDEZ: Old people and infants naturally repeat things; they may be good carriers.

GRANT MAZZY: Carriers for what? For what? Ken? Ken?

KEN LONEY: *(voice-over)* I'm gonna try . . .

GRANT MAZZY: Can you think?

KEN LONEY: *(voice-over)* I can.

DR. MENDEZ: Yes. Stick to simple questions. Simple.

KEN LONEY: *(voice-over)* Simple. Simple. Simple. Simple. Simple.

DR. MENDEZ: That is it. He is gone. What you hear is him. He is a crude radio signal now. He's seeking.

KEN LONEY: *(voice-over)* Simple. Simple. Simple.

SYDNEY BRIAR: Do we leave him on?

GRANT MAZZY: I don't know. Do we leave him on?

DR. MENDEZ: No, he's transmitting. No. It's not a safe sound. Turn him off.

SYDNEY BRIAR: I'm turning him off. Goodbye, Ken.

GRANT MAZZY: Goodbye, Ken.

KEN LONEY: *(voice-over)* Simple. Simple. Simple. Simple.

KEN keeps repeating "simple" under the following dialogue.

DR. MENDEZ: I have an idea what we have.

GRANT MAZZY: Ken? C'mon, Ken.

SYDNEY BRIAR: He's gonna start killing people. Is he? Turn him off now.

GRANT MAZZY: Ken's a good man, Syd. Ken's a good man. Jesus. We all know Ken.

SYDNEY BRIAR: And now we all have to say goodbye. Our man in the Sunshine Chopper.

GRANT MAZZY: Goodbye, Ken. From all of us. Everyone listening. Can you hear me, Ken?

SYDNEY turns off her phone. Silence.

DR. MENDEZ: He's gone. Well, he's gone SOMEWHERE, I mean. He's a little noise now, a homicidal little sound or two.

SYDNEY is suppressing terrible sobs. She is near a complete breakdown but holding on. MENDEZ notices this and motions to GRANT, who moves to comfort her.

GRANT MAZZY: I'm sorry, Syd. Ken was your friend, wasn't he?

SYDNEY withdraws slightly from GRANT's hand.

SYDNEY BRIAR: He wasn't a friend. Ken Loney was a pedophile. Not a pedophile. We never trusted him around our kids. And I've known him for seventeen years. That's all.

SYDNEY wipes her eyes and takes a deep breath.

A long, long time.

Long silence.

Shit. That's not a very good obituary.

GRANT MAZZY: Especially for a guy with a Dodge Dart.

GRANT, DR. MENDEZ, and SYDNEY look out at the bloodied LAUREL ANN. She is even more gory than before—hideous— and now moves as though sickly, twitchy but leaden. She makes her way to the sound booth window.

Sorry. Folks. Uh . . . we're still here. We're just . . . Laurel Ann has joined us again. She's staring at us. She looks worse. Her forehead is now . . .

SYDNEY BRIAR: Stop.

DR. MENDEZ: You're sure she can't hear us?

SYDNEY BRIAR: Nope. Nothing.

GRANT MAZZY: Can they read lips?

DR. MENDEZ: Good question.

SYDNEY BRIAR: *(whispering)* She's going.

The three exhale loudly. MENDEZ *pops another pill.*

DR. MENDEZ: Read lips.

GRANT MAZZY: Sorry, Doctor?

DR. MENDEZ: It's just a very interesting thing you have said. Can they read lips?

GRANT MAZZY: Really? Interesting how? I remind our listeners that we are talking to Dr. John Mendez who . . .

DR. MENDEZ: It can't be! It can't be! It's impossible!

GRANT *stops talking at the outburst.* SYDNEY *leans in.*

SYDNEY BRIAR: What's impossible, Doctor?

MENDEZ'S *eyes are wide with fear and wonder. He has had a revelation.*

He puts his fingers to his lips as he thinks. Then he draws himself up and starts talking very softly. GRANT *and* SYDNEY *lean in close to listen.*

DR. MENDEZ: *(whispering)* It is an infection. It is viral, that much is clear. But not of the blood.

MENDEZ continues in a hushed voice full of breathless drama.

Not blood. Not in the air. Not on or even in our bodies. But here . . .

MENDEZ stops cryptically.

GRANT MAZZY: Where?

DR. MENDEZ: It's in words. Not all words. Not all speaking. But in some. Some words are infected.

GRANT and SYDNEY hold their breath. The silence is protracted and dreadful.

And it spreads out when the contaminated word is spoken, like a sneeze.

GRANT MAZZY: *(whispering)* A sneeze?

DR. MENDEZ continues talking in a hushed tone.

DR. MENDEZ: We are at the deep-sea heat vents; we are witnessing the emergence of a new arrangement for life and our language is its host. Maybe your cat poster was the superheated vent, maybe it sprung spontaneously out of a perception, maybe it laid in wait in our coincidences, recognizing, mirroring. It may be boundless. It may be infinite. It may be a god bug.

GRANT MAZZY: Dr. Mendez. I don't even believe in UFOs so I'm having a hard time—

DR. MENDEZ: Really? That's sensible because there are no UFOs. But I assure you that a monster is bouncing through your language frantically trying to keep its host alive. Look at what happened to Ken.

GRANT and SYDNEY blink, trying to comprehend.

GRANT MAZZY: Is this transmission itself . . .

DR. MENDEZ: If this bug enters us, it does not enter by making contact with our eardrums. It enters us when we hear a word and understand it. Understand? Once it is understood, the virus takes hold. It copies itself in our understanding.

MENDEZ thinks for a moment before speaking.

There is something else. Something I should tell you. When I was outside in the snow. Hiding. I saw something in the sky. It was the sun. The sun itself had turned into something else. It was still burning, a dark light, but it was not the sun. It was a burning barn. Not just any barn. I had seen this barn, it was a barn I pass by on the road and it was up high in the heavens on fire. So. I see this. I see this and I think, because this is the question: Am I getting this crazy sickness? Yes. Yes. This is what I think. And then I see across the street between two cars, there are two children and they are looking up and pointing at the sun. And I knew then that I wasn't hallucinating. It was a hallucination but it wasn't mine. It was reality that was hallucinating. The bug is leaping from language to a new host; it has found the great and original copy machine. The host is everything. Boom. The great domain that keeps us is getting very very ill and may well die.

GRANT MAZZY: Should we even be talking about this? Should we be talking at all?

SYDNEY BRIAR: Talking about what, Grant? Talking about what exactly?

DR. MENDEZ: To be safe. No. Probably not. Talking is risky. Um. And yes. Talk radio is high-risk, I would say. So, we should stop.

GRANT MAZZY: I think we need to tell people this. We need to tell people. We have to get this out.

DR. MENDEZ: It's your call, Mr. Mazzy. Let's just hope that what you're getting out isn't destroying your world.

A very long silence. MENDEZ *sneezes and pops another pill. Loud breathing. Slowly in then out.*

The whole world can hear you breathing.

GRANT *pulls himself back from the mic and turns it off.*

No. It's fine. You're breathing. That's your top news story.

SYDNEY BRIAR: Go to Muzak. Muzak. Key in fourteen.

GRANT *pushes some buttons.*

DR. MENDEZ: It seems like we're still talking. Should we make the moratorium official?

A phone rings.

GRANT MAZZY: Here she comes!

Crash! LAUREL ANN collides with the booth.

SYDNEY BRIAR: Lulu? Is that you?

SYDNEY gasps. Her daughter.

Hi. Honey. Why are you calling mommy at work?

A heavy crash shakes the booth.

Are you okay? Is Daddy there? Can I talk to him for sec? I know, honey. I know. Are you still in the city? Good.

Horrible slamming.

No. Mommy didn't forget. I was going to call on my coffee break, sweetheart.

DR. MENDEZ: She shouldn't be just talking to anybody who calls. No sweetheart, please.

SYDNEY BRIAR: Not right now. It's not a good time. Can I talk to . . . Honey, please. It's not your birthday, sweetie. It's Valentine's Day.

A terrible crash that makes SYDNEY jump. She is terrified and crying, trying to sound normal.

Happy Valentines Day to you. Happy Valentines Day to you. Happy Valentine's Day dear . . . Lulu . . . Lulu? Hello? Shit.

SYDNEY breathes with heavy emotion.

Kids are okay. Okay. Okay.

The phone's dead again.

There is silence in and outside the booth.

What . . . what is that on the glass?

DR. MENDEZ: That's some of Laurel Ann. Something strange is happening to her. I haven't seen this.

This is new. We're going to see what happens. I think we're seeing something new.

MENDEZ acknowledges SYDNEY, who is suffering for her friend.

I'm sorry, yes. This is awful. You are in shock.

GRANT MAZZY: I didn't give her that stupid Valentine's Day card. I should have . . . I just . . .

DR. MENDEZ: Oh . . . that makes this worse. I agree. I'm sorry. This is very sad for you.

SYDNEY BRIAR: I liked my card. I didn't tell you. I'm sorry.

GRANT looks at SYDNEY.

DR. MENDEZ: Yes. That's good. You should be a comfort to each other. Oh. What's this now?

> *LAUREL ANN is grunting rhythmically, like a cat heaving a hairball. Then the sound of a terrible water explosion as LAUREL ANN's upper torso explodes.*

> *SYDNEY collapses and starts gagging. GRANT supports her and holds her as she throws up. She gasps.*

That is new. That's what happens when the victim cannot find a victim. This is the fate they are trying to escape. My god that was impressive.

> *Noticing GRANT and SYDNEY.*

Yes. No. And, singularly monstrous. Defies comprehension. I'm sorry.

> *MENDEZ goes silent. SYDNEY is sobbing into GRANT's chest.*

SYDNEY BRIAR: Let's get the fuck outta here.

> *SYDNEY kicks the door.*

GRANT MAZZY: Okay with me.

DR. MENDEZ: No. No. No. This is the same situation I had at my office. There are probably hundreds pressed to the walls of this building.

GRANT holds SYDNEY more tightly. MENDEZ frowns.

What we need is a flame-thrower.

GRANT MAZZY: I thought we weren't supposed to talk.

DR. MENDEZ: What? Oh right. Right.

SYDNEY BRIAR: In French. We can speak in French. *Parler français.*

GRANT MAZZY: *En français.*

DR. MENDEZ: *En français.*

I don't speak French!

SYDNEY BRIAR: *Il sera exposé.*

GRANT MAZZY: *Il va nous exposer.*

MENDEZ starts speaking in Armenian. He continues what sounds like an emotional argument with himself.

SYDNEY BRIAR: *Qu'est-il en train de faire? Que dit-il?*

GRANT MAZZY: *Je ne sais pas. Allons-y.*

What are you saying?

MENDEZ's rant is getting more intense and GRANT and SYDNEY are starting to panic.

SYDNEY BRIAR: *En français! En français!*

GRANT MAZZY: *Il va souffler! C'est Laurel Ann tout encore. Il parle en arrière je pense!*

SYDNEY BRIAR: *Qu'est-ce qu'on fait?! Qu'est-ce qu'on fait?!*

GRANT MAZZY: *Je ne sais pas! Tue-le!*

SYDNEY BRIAR: *Vous le tuez!*

DR. MENDEZ: It's only the English language that's infected!

SYDNEY BRIAR: *C'est tout.*

There's a struggle, MENDEZ growling like an animal. Then the terrible steady thump of something stabbing flesh.

Heavy breathing.

GRANT MAZZY: *Vous l'avez tué, Syd.*

Silence, then a gasp from SYDNEY.

SYDNEY BRIAR: Oh my god. We don't know for sure! Grant! Do we know that he was sick? Do we know?

GRANT MAZZY: *En français! Français!*

SYDNEY BRIAR: How can we find out? I have to know, Grant! I just killed somebody!

SYDNEY is now panicking and GRANT fears losing control of the situation.

GRANT MAZZY: *En français, Syd! S'il vous plaît!*

SYDNEY turns on GRANT.

SYDNEY BRIAR: Why didn't you do it? Why did I have to do it? I just killed a perfectly healthy man because he was talking in another language? Grant, why did you let me!

The sounds of struggle. SYDNEY's voice is muffled as GRANT puts his hand over her face.

Don't touch me, Grant! Listen to me! Listen!

Her voice becomes increasingly muffled until finally we hear stifled screams, then a terrible silence.

The silence sits for a while, then a loud jingle. A commercial shatters the silence. When it's over another silence.

The sound of a deep breath taken in then exhaled.

GRANT MAZZY: Grant Mazzy here, Pontypool. Don't know who's out there. Whether you're listening to this or . . . eating your radios. But I'm here and so are you. Whoever, whatever you are. I'm going to go right to some . . . fresh . . . obituaries. Laurel Ann Drummond died today. But you knew that already.

Pause.

You were here. And Dr. John Mendez died today. Some of you may have tried to kill him yourself, earlier today. Well, we managed to do that ourselves. The headline might read, "Interview gone horribly wrong." Anyway, we say goodbye to the good doctor. And the next one . . . this, probably the last obituary you will hear on this radio, is different. Different because it's someone who meant a lot to me. Sydney Briar died today. And I killed her. Not the same way I imagine you're killing people today. Or being killed. No. She was murdered. But you can't stop someone from talking without stopping them from breathing. And so I tried to do one thing and just ended up doing it all. And so, here I am, at the end of everything, the cockroach that fled into the radio, waiting to see what, if anything, happens now.

I should tell you that I started to notice something strange a while ago and I decided I'm going to, as long as I can, I'm going to stay alive by talking. I feel drawn right now to the word "paper." I don't feel compelled to say it. Yet. But I can feel it sitting there like an itch. I have an infected word and it will spread. Soon all I'll want to say is "paper."

> GRANT *continues but appears to be disappearing. All the grey tones begin to disappear. His image becomes very contrasty. Just blacks and whites. Moving toward abstract lines.*

There, see? I felt that. To say that word, "paper." Like my hand brushed over it and for a second, relief. Paper. Wonder when I heard it? Who said it to me? Paper. I am here.

It's weird. I feel . . . I feel like I'm being hunted. Like something's . . . something's looking for me. Sitting there, making a little hunter's bluff out of a word, but I know the word. I can . . . avoid the word. I can circle the word. Or I can . . . oh . . . what was that? Something else moved in there. Something's trying to erase me. Each word. There's another. Each word that it takes I get . . . smaller. I have to be somewhere. I have to get somewhere. Is it safe? Am I here, in this voice? A collection of words, safe ones, do they have to describe me? I'm being chased. It takes me in the things I say. In the words, I think. It's not safe to be what I say. Where am I? Shit. Where am I? I feel like I'm running away but how can I be something. I have to be something fast. Now. Something that is small. Something you can't find. You can't read. Not read. I have to be something you don't understand.

GRANT stops and grunts.

Talk to me.

He moans.

Talk to me.

GRANT inhales sharply.

Syd?

GRANT sits silently in the booth.

Syd.

GRANT sits in grieving silence.

That's what. That's what. Over a word. Through a letter. That's crazy. Crazy. A memory. A feeling. You don't understand this. This is fuckin' poison. Somewhere in my life. Something I barely remember. Make a faint, faint bridge then cross. Cross.

He frantically wipes his face as he talks in a manic ramble.

Does it come by wind? Should I be low? On my side? I need to not be here or I will be found. I was five years old when I saw her. What was her name? Anna. I remember. Her name was Anna. And she sat with three other girls at a separate table. Sun streaming through the window. And we were supposed to draw our houses, but I wanted to draw Anna. I wanted her to know how much I wanted to draw her.

A saturated light in a room. A girl at a desk. She is smiling.
SYDNEY.

I got up, just a little boy leaving his seat to walk five steps away but it was bigger than all the world, took longer than anything ever had before.

A wide black line through white.

I walked over and watched her draw. Her hand pulled crayon down. The teacher was asking me something, and other children, but then the thick line appeared and the blue window.

A blue square, crudely drawn, vibrating with colour.

And her wide honey-yellow sun with seven rays that shone down on Anna's house on the paper. That little stone cat. I remember! I remember. It was white but she made it blue that day. And she made the bridge out of the same honey as the sun.

We focus on the surface of the paper, white fibres.

Ahh. There. Beside the line. So far back. Hiding here. This isn't a word. This isn't me. You can't find me here. I'm barely in a memory I barely remember and do not understand. This is least. I'm a thing that may not have even happened on paper that may not have been. Hiding. Paper. Paper. Paper.

A soft, sad moan.

Paper. Paper. Shit. Trap.

Black.

ACKNOWLEDGEMENTS

Much thanks to Annie Gibson, Blake Sproule, and Mandy Bayrami. Also Anderson Lawfer and all the companies that have mounted this little nightmare. Thanks all.

Toronto-born Tony Burgess is a playwright, screenwriter, and novelist. His most notable works include *The Hellmouths of Bewdley*, *Pontypool Changes Everything*, *Caesarea*, and *Pontypool*, the screenplay for the film adaptation of the novel. Tony lives in Stayner, Ontario.

First edition: October 2015
Printed and bound in Canada by Imprimerie Gauvin, Gatineau

Author photograph by Matt Wiele
Cover art and by Justin Erickson

**PLAYWRIGHTS
CANADA PRESS**

202-269 Richmond Street West
Toronto, ON
M5V 1X1

416.703.0013
info@playwrightscanada.com
playwrightscanada.com
@playcanpress

A **bundled** eBook edition is available
with the purchase of this print book.

CLEARLY PRINT YOUR NAME ABOVE IN UPPER CASE

Instructions to claim your eBook edition:
1. Download the BitLit app for Android or iOS
2. Write your name in **UPPER CASE** above
3. Use the BitLit app to submit a photo
4. Download your eBook to any device